ABOUT WALT DISNEY ANIMATION STUDIOS ARTIST SHOWCASE BOOKS

THIS SERIES OF ORIGINAL PICTURE BOOKS PUTS THE SPOTLIGHT ON THE INCREDIBLE ARTISTS OF WALT DISNEY ANIMATION STUDIOS. THE PAGES OF EACH BOOK SHOWCASE THE PERSONAL WORK OF ONE OF THESE TALENTED ARTISTS AND INTRODUCE A BRAND-NEW WORLD AND CHARACTERS.

CATCH MY BREATH

WRITTEN & ILLUSTRATED BY PAUL BRIGGS

Disney · HYPERION

LOS ANGELES   NEW YORK

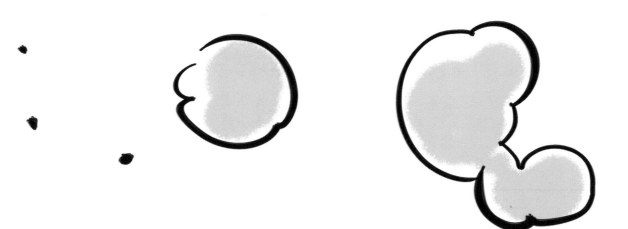

WHERE WOULD IT GO?!

MOM SAYS GRANDPA GRUMBLES
UNDER HIS BREATH.....

MAYBE MY BREATH
IS THERE?

MY BROTHER TELLS ME I HAVE DOG BREATH.....
MAYBE MY BREATH IS IN
T-BONE'S MOUTH?

MY BREATH IS SWIMMING IN THE SEA?
IT'S WAITING WITH BATED BREATH,
ABOUT TO BE NIBBLED!

EXCUSE ME,

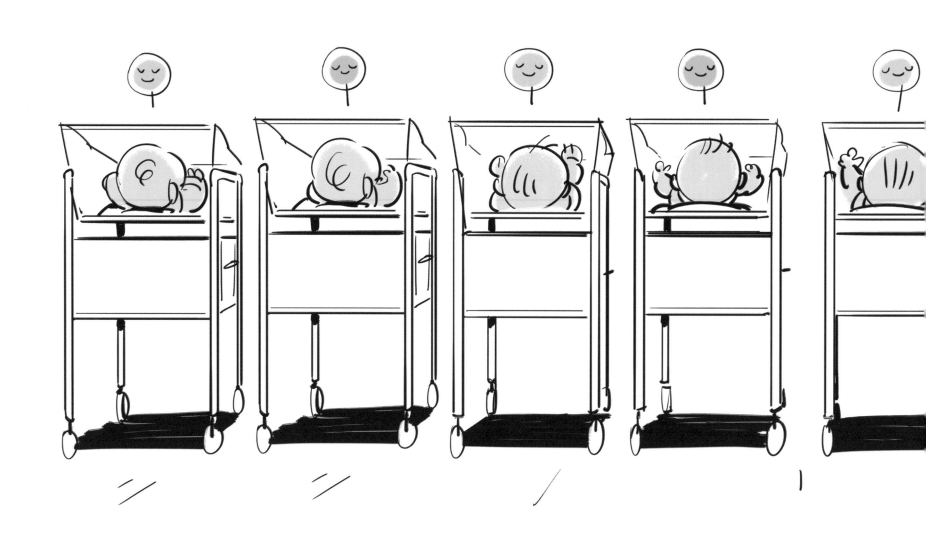

I'LL NEVER BE ABLE TO CATCH MY BREATH.

I WILL NEVER LOSE MY BREATH AGAIN.

FOR THE ONES WHO TAKE MY BREATH AWAY—

MY MOTHER, CHRISTIN, LEO & LUKE

AUTHOR'S NOTE

I WORK AT AN AMAZING PLACE —
WALT DISNEY ANIMATION STUDIOS —

DISNEY HAS CREATED TIMELESS VERSIONS OF CLASSICS LIKE *SNOW WHITE AND THE SEVEN DWARFS*, *BAMBI*, AND *PINOCCHIO*. EVERY DAY I COME TO WORK, I GET TO BE A PART OF A NEW GENERATION OF FILMMAKERS WHO ARE CREATING THE MEMORABLE STORIES AND CHARACTERS OF TODAY, LIKE ANNA AND ELSA, HIRO AND BAYMAX, AND MANY MORE.

BUT THE GREATEST JOY I EXPERIENCE AT WALT DISNEY ANIMATION STUDIOS IS WHEN WE'RE ALL SHARING IDEAS.

IDEAS FLOW THROUGHOUT THE BUILDING, LIKE MILLIONS OF FIREFLIES. THE BEST IDEAS ARE CAPTURED AND MADE INTO ANIMATED FILMS. ONE DAY, A LITTLE FIREFLY OF AN IDEA SPRUNG UP IN ME.

ENTER THE WALT DISNEY ANIMATION STUDIOS ARTIST SHOWCASE—

A SPECIAL PROGRAM WHERE ANIMATORS LIKE ME CAN SHARE AN IDEA, AND, IF SELECTED, DEVELOP IT INTO A PICTURE BOOK, LIKE *CATCH MY BREATH*.

I HAD RECENTLY EXPERIENCED THE BIRTHS OF MY TWO AMAZING SONS AND THE PASSING OF MY BEAUTIFUL MOTHER. I WAS MOVED TO WITNESS FIRST BREATHS OF LIFE AND A LAST BREATH OF LIFE, AND IT MADE ME SEE BREATH IN A NEW LIGHT. BREATH IS OUR BEST FRIEND AND WITH US LONGER THAN ANYTHING ELSE.

IT'S A GREAT PROGRAM THAT I THINK WALT DISNEY HIMSELF WOULD HAVE LOVED, BECAUSE IT CELEBRATES TWO THINGS HE HELD DEAR:

IT STRUCK ME HOW THERE ARE SO MANY FUN SAYINGS ABOUT BREATH.

THAT'S WHEN I CAME UP WITH *CATCH MY BREATH*. BUT THERE WAS A PROBLEM—IT DIDN'T SEEM LIKE THE RIGHT IDEA FOR AN ANIMATED FILM.

IDEAS AND THE POWER OF THE IMAGINATIONS OF ARTISTS.

FIRST EDITION, SEPTEMBER 2017

10 9 8 7 6 5 4 3 2 1

FAC-019817-17216

PRINTED IN MALAYSIA

THIS BOOK IS SET IN ADORN CONDENSED SANS

DESIGNED BY SCOTT PIEHL

ILLUSTRATIONS CREATED DIGITALLY

LIBRARY OF CONGRESS CATALOGING-IN-PUBLICATION DATA

NAMES: BRIGGS, PAUL, AUTHOR, ILLUSTRATOR.

TITLE: CATCH MY BREATH / PAUL BRIGGS.

DESCRIPTION: LOS ANGELES ; NEW YORK : DISNEY*HYPERION, [2017] | SERIES:

WALT DISNEY ANIMATION STUDIOS ARTIST SHOWCASE | SUMMARY: A CHILD EXPLORES

WHERE BREATH MIGHT GO AFTER IT IS LOST, WHETHER UNDER SOMEONE ELSE'S BREATH, AMONG A NURSERY'S BABY'S BREATH,

OR IN A BREATH OF FRESH AIR. INCLUDES FACTS ABOUT IDIOMS AND THE WALT DISNEY ANIMATION STUDIOS ARTIST SHOWCASE.

IDENTIFIERS: LCCN 2016057811 | ISBN 9781484728376

SUBJECTS: | CYAC: RESPIRATION--FICTION. | ENGLISH

LANGUAGE--IDIOMS--FICTION.

CLASSIFICATION: LCC PZ7.1.B7547 CAT 2017 | DDC [E]--DC23

LC RECORD AVAILABLE AT HTTPS://LCCN.LOC.GOV/2016057811

REINFORCED BINDING

VISIT WWW.DISNEYBOOKS.COM

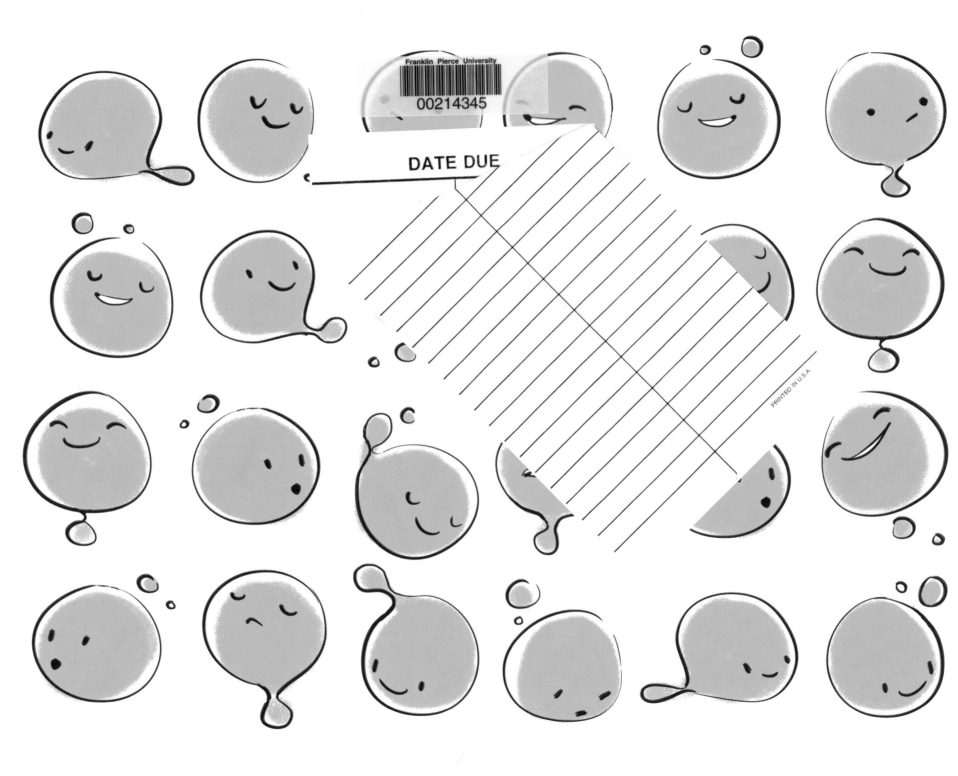

DATE DUE